THERE STILL ARE
BUFFALO

by Ann Nolan Clark

Illustrations by
Stephen Tongier

Ancient City Press
Santa Fe, New Mexico

First published in 1942 by the Bureau of Indian Affairs

International Standard Book Number: 0-941270-67-X

Book design by Mary Powell

Cover illustration by Tim Green

Illustrations by Stephen Tongier

First Ancient City Press Printing

Library of Congress Cataloging-in-Publication Data

Clark, Ann Nolan, 1898-
    There still are buffalo / Ann Nolan Clark ; illustrated by Steve
Tongier.
        p.   cm.
    Summary: A buffalo bull baby is born in the land of the Sioux and
cared for by his mother, learns from the herd, and grows to become
its leader.
    ISBN 0-941270-67-X (pbk.)
    1. Bison — Juvenile fiction.   [1. Bison — Fiction.]   I. Tongier,
Steve, ill.   II. Title.
PZ10.3.C54Th   1991
[E] — dc20   90-85645
                                                           CIP
                                                           AC

10   9   8   7   6   5   4   3   2   1

— 1 —

In the Dakotas, the Indian country,
the Sioux People have set aside
a tract of their precious range land—
a rolling plain of grass land,
ravines and creeks—
that the antelope and the deer
and the elk herds
may roam again
upon the earth;
that the buffalo
may live again
in splendid right.

And buffalo live there
    on this range land,
    resting and grazing,
    going to water,
    going to new grass,
    using the same old trails,
    using the same old ways
    that buffalo have used
    since the Beginning.

The Indians
    who keep them know.

There still are buffalo.

A little noise
  breaks the silence
  of the ravine.
A whisper of movement
  breaks the stillness.

What is it
  that breaks so lightly
  into a dream of quiet?
What is it
  that steps so bravely
  into a new world?

A buffalo cow rises heavily
  from her bed in the trampled grasses
  and lightly,
  like an eagle's wing
  brushing the face of the sun,
  breathes softly
  upon her new-born baby.

The breath of her life
    flows strongly
    from her wide, black nostrils,
    flows warmly
    against the wetness of her calf.

A little bull buffalo baby is born.
The buffalo mother nurses her baby.
She licks him gently.
Lovingly she nudges him.
Lovingly she nudges him,
    coaxing him, coaxing him
    to get up, to stand up,
    to face the wind.

The buffalo baby
    is little and scrawny,
    is short-haired and fuzzy
    and as reddish and tow-colored
    as the sun-scorched grasses
    that make his bed.

He boasts no flowing beard
    nor shaggy mane,
    no high-arched shoulders
    nor curving horns.

He does not stand
   in splendid strength
   against the sky.

Can it be
   this small one
   will grow
   in strength and power?

Can it be
   this small one
   will be Chief
   of the Thundering Herd?

Day flows by
   like the water in the creek bed
   flows onward.

The buffalo mother stands
   facing the wind.
She is guarding her baby.

Gray dawn
   stretches its wings
   over the plains country.

The buffalo mother stands patiently
   facing the wind.
She is guarding her baby.

The little bull buffalo
   is strong for a baby.

In two or three days
   his sturdy, thick legs
   carry him upward
   to walk near his mother
   as she climbs the steep sides
   of the sheltered ravine
   to join the herd on the table land
   where they are grazing.

— 3 —

Patches of snow
 still cover the table land.
Early spring winds
 blow over the plains land.
The buffalo herd moves onward,
 grazing and resting
 chewing and chewing,
 drinking and wallowing,
 moving on, moving on,
 following the leader.

The herd mother goes first
 wise in her leadership.
Next come the cows and calves,
 the spike-horns and yearlings
 and lastly the bulls,
 the chief and his guardsmen,
 ruler and protectors,
 proud in their strength,
 their bravery and beauty,
 proud in their work
 of keeping the herd
 banded closely together.

Buffalo are wild and free,
    but they have ways
    which they must follow
    which are as deep and unchanging
    as their zigzag trails.

All through the summer
    the little calf follows his mother,
    nursing and sleeping
    grazing and growing.

His tow-colored body
   becomes red-tinged
   like the short grass
   in autumn.
His thick hair curls
   at the base of his little knob horns.

His body grows fuller.
His legs become thicker.
His new coat is darker
   and coarser and longer.

The little knobs of horns
   grow out straight,
   solid little handles
   on his bony head.

Who is there to say
   that this small one
   may not, some day,
   be Chief of the Herd!

— 4 —

Once,
  the herd became frightened
  at the quick coming
  of a summer storm.
Blindly, they ran
  from this unknown terror
  that they felt about them
  in the quickening
  of the wind.

Tongier '91

Blindly they ran,
    snorting, panting,
    their great bodies
    crashing together.
Their shaggy heads swung
    this way, and that way,
    as their white-mooned, near-sighted eyes
    hunted an opening in the thick cloud
    of dust and moving brown bodies.

It was a stampede,
    a wild terror-filled stampede.
The little calf lost his mother.

Did he bellow in fright?
Did he run under the hoofs
    of the running herd?

No!
Not this small one!
He was a true buffalo baby.
He hid his head in a bush.
He stood quietly, hiding his head,
    thinking, because he could not see
    he could not be seen.

Only his little rump showed.
Only his little tail twitched
   to show that he was
   just a little afraid.

After awhile the stampeding buffalo
   stopped in their flight,
   rested, became calm,
   turned back to graze.

All this time the buffalo cow
   had been hunting through the dust cloud
   for her little lost calf.
Her wide, black nostrils
   sniffed in the wind
   for his scent.

At last she traced him
   to his hiding place.
She pushed him gently
   out of his bush.
She licked him and nosed him.

He walked proudly near her,
   pawing the earth,
   his baby tail sticking straight up.

He walked proudly near her,
    charging the clumps of weeds
    that grew in his way.
He stood by her side
    chewing his cud,
    facing the wind
    and feeling brave.

— 5 —

Once
    the range riders,
    the Indian cowboys,
    tried to drive the buffalo
    into new pasture.

They ran the herd hard.
They confused and frightened them.
They circled and turned them
    using their strongest and fastest,
    their best-trained curring ponies.

The great beasts ran
    in terror, in panic.

18

Their shaggy heads lowered
  to bring their near-sighted eyes
  close to the ground.

A young calf fell forward,
  went down to the ground
  under the death-pounding hooves
  of the running herd,
  of the terror blind herd.

A wide gate was opened
  in the fence of the new pasture.
Beyond, the grass waved high.
No living thing
  broke the peace
  of empty quiet.
Through the gate lay safety
  and healing quiet.
Through the gate lay peace
  from the hard-riding cowboys.

The yelling cowboys,
  the pursuing cowboys
  closed in upon the herd
  bringing them nearer
  to the opening
  into the new pasture.

19

But the lead cow turned,
    swerved past the opening,
    refusing to be driven.

She, having always led,
    held to her leadership
    and the following herd
    true to its instincts
    turned also.

They could not be driven.

Again and again,
    year after year,
    the cowboys tried
    to drive the herd
    into new pasture.

Again and again
    the lead cow turned
    and the others followed.

Is it not right
    that the old Indians
    gave reverence
    to the buffalo
    which had greater strength
    than man?

— 6 —

The seasons move swiftly,
   spring and summer,
   autumn and winter.

The calf stays with his mother.
She watches him,
   she nurses him.
He follows her
   wherever she goes.

Little by little he learns
   to find his own food,
   to fight his enemies,
   to swim in the deep holes
   in the creek,
   to bathe in the dust beds
   of the wallows,
   to care for himself.

When a new calf is born,
   the buffalo mother
   has the new one to care for.
She cannot spend her time
   with last year's baby.

He is a yearling now.
He goes with the herd
    in a place of his own.

He stays with the other yearlings,
    using his new-found strength
    to push them with his young, shaggy head.
He faces the wind, smelling it,
    listening to its song.

The young yearling
    looks with wonder
    at the grass-covered plains
    and the rolling hills.

He sees the antelope and the deer
   rush by, swift as the wind,
   frightened by their own fear.

He sees an elk herd
   bounding and crashing
   through the trees
   along the creek bed,
   bounding and crashing,
   their heads held back,
   their great antlers
   branched against the sky.

He stops to look, to smell,
   to listen to the world
   that is around him,
There is something
   but the guard bulls
   nose him onward.

He must not be left behind,
   straggling, undefended.
He must keep to his place
   in the moving herd.

The yearling's horns begin to curve.
Slowly his shoulders arch
  higher and higher.
He is no longer a calf
  following his mother.
He is no longer a yearling
  to be kept in his place.
He is now a spike-horn.

— 7 —

The seasons come
  like enemy bands.
Warrior seasons
  counting coup
  upon each defeated,
  passing season.

Winter is a gray wolf
  howling the death call
  into the bleakness of cold!

Now snowflakes frozen to roundness
  dance to the wind in whirling patterns
  across the gray faces of the hardened drifts.

Moon Mother from the folds of night blanket
   bathes the unbroken whiteness of the land
   with the silver foam of her light.

Shaggy buffalo covered with hoar frost
   are walking snowdrifts
   through the wind-blown snow.

This is winter in the buffalo country.

A blinding blizzard lashes in fury
   the great beasts of the plains.

The young spike-horn
   stands in the drifting snow.
When hunger stabs him
   like the lance of a hunter,
   he gets down heavily
   upon his knees
   and with his half-grown beard
   sweeps the snow from the grass.

He eats the snow-covered grass
   in great mouthfuls,
   then rests tiredly
   in the place where he has eaten.

There is something
    about snow-covered grass
    that is good for the buffalo.
It helps them to keep fat
    and to keep their courage
    and their strength.

The sun follows the blizzard
    gently undoing
    the work of the angered winds.

Patches of grass
    uncovered
    by the snow's melting
    dare bravely
    to stand on tiptoe,
    reaching upward for warmth.

— 8 —

Spring is an impish coyote
    playing tricks
    with the weather.

Spring rains flood the creeks
   and fill the buffalo wallows.
Spring dust storms cover the land
   in choking clouds of black dust.

The buffalo trails run crookedly
   up the hills
   in faint lines of new green.

This is spring in the buffalo country.

The spike-horn's winter robe
   falls out in great patches
   leaving his shaggy coat
   faded to mud color, dull and bare
   like the burned places
   of a prairie fire.

Winged insects sting him
   like the flickings of arrows.
Winged insects torture him
   into a frenzy.

For who can battle
   small things
   that cannot be seen?

The young bull rubs his itching sides
   against the cottonwoods
   in the creek bottoms
   leaving them shining and smooth
   with a glistening polish.

He digs deep in the melting snow pools
   making a mud wallow
   to cool his pain.

Spring is an impish coyote
   playing in the wind
   and tossing the weather
   like a tumbleweed ball.

— 9 —

Summer is a red bird
   flame feathered
   in its winged flight
   earthward.

Rock pines darken
   the folds of the hills.
Tall grasses outline
   the water courses.

Heat lightning flames
   in the distant sky.
Heat haze dances
   in the yellow spaces.

This is summer in the buffalo country.

The bulls are fat and restless.
They paw the floor of the ravine
   trampling the bruised grass,
   tearing the wounded earth
   out-thundering the thunder.

The rutting season is near.
The fighting season is near.
The bulls are fat and restless.

The young bull is now full grown.
He stands as tall as a tall man.
He weighs more than ten tall men.
He runs like the wind,
   panting and blowing.

Now is his time
   to step forward
   in his place
   as Herd Father.

The young bull is now full grown
    his hind quarters are brown
    as the tobacco
    in the peace pipes
    of the Indians.

His hump is yellow
    as the dry grass
    on the hillsides.

Now is his time
    to step forward
    in his place
    as Buffalo Chieftain.

The young bull is now full grown.
His mane is deep brown
    as the bare earth
    under the pine trees.

His face and horns
    and hoofs and beard
    and tasseled tail
    are black as the night sky.

The north wind is in his breath.
The flaming sun is in his blood.

His pride lies
    in the strength of his shaggy head
    and curving horns and muscled shoulders;
    in his scars that show the battles
    he has fought and won;
    in the size of his herd
    and his place within it.

In these things lies his pride.
He has strength.
He has bravery.

— 10 —

Autumn is wild geese flying
    in a winged arrow tip
    across the sky.

Birds fly southward
    and thin ice
    coats the running water in the creek.

This is autumn in the buffalo country.

The young bull stands
  on the hilltop.
Bravely, he stands.
His black nostrils widening
  to the force of the wind.
His near-sighted eyes
  gazing unseeing
  into the unknown.

He is the son of the Great Mystery
  following the buffalo trails,
  following the buffalo ways
  across the miles
  and across the years.

He is the son of the Great Mystery.
Deep in his heart
  lies the memory of battle,
  the memory of the stalking gray wolf,
  the crouching mountain lion,
  the swarms of men
  shooting him down
  for the sport of chase.

His trails are cut deep
   in his heart
   in the land.

— 11 —

Now, the young buffalo
   is ten years old.
Ten times the seasons
   have passed him
   since he climbed the ravine
   by the side of his mother.
Ten times he has faced
   the summer heat,
   the autumn winds,
   the winter blizzards,
   the spring dust storms.

He is ten years old.

He has listened to the whisperings
   of his heart.
He has listened to the teachings
   of the herd.

He has taken his turn
  as sentinel
  on the lonely hilltop
  as the rest of the herd
  drank the cool waters
  of the running creek.

He has taken his turn
  as guard
  on the flanks of the herd
  crowding the cows and calves
  into the center
  where they would be safe
  when danger threatened.

He has chased the coyote
  over the plains.

He has chased the lone rider
    over the hills.
He has charged the enemy
    wherever he met it.

He has fought his way up
    among the young bulls.
Now he steps forward
    to fight the Herd Father.

All the young bulls circle,
    horning one another,
    but facing the center
    of the ring
    to watch.

The cows stop feeding.
They stand in little groups
    chewing their cuds
    and watching the ring.

The earth trembles
    to the fury
    of the fighting bulls.

The earth shakes
    to the poundings
    of their stamping hoofs.

Dust rose in a thick cloud
   as the two bulls
   tore the heart from the earth
   and threw it
   powdered to dust
   against the sky.

At last the old bull
   is defeated.

The young bull is now
   the Buffalo Father.
He is now the Head Chief
   of the thundering Herd.

He guards the stragglers
   and protects the weak ones.
He does not allow
   cows and yearlings to stray.
He does not allow
   new bulls to come in.
He keeps his band
   herded closely together,
   for he is the Head Chief,
   he is the Father.

He directs the herd movement
   and the herd defense.
The old bulls are the outposts
   away from the herd.
The young bulls are the flank guards
   on the edge of the herd.

Every few days he visits
   the outposts and the guards
   to make certain
   that they are doing
   what he wills them to do.

He takes the first drink
   at the creek,
   the best grazing place,
   the first long bath
   in the buffalo wallow.

He is the Chief!

He steps proudly
   that all may know
   he is the Buffalo Father.

He is the Chief of the Thundering Herd.

— 12 —

The years pass by.

An open winter is followed
   by a rainless spring.
Hot winds blow over the land.
Summer comes in wearily
   in dry, heat-tortured despair.

There is no water in the wallows.
There is no water in the creek bed.
There is no water in the cloudless sky,
   in the barren land,
   in the never-stopping winds.

The buffalo roam the land,
   following their crooked trails,
   their white eyes bloodshot,
   their wide nostrils blood rimmed,
   hunting, hunting
   for a blade of living green,
   for a drop of living water.

There is no rain.

There is no rain.

— 13 —

The years blow by
  on the wings of the wind.
The years pass by.

The buffalo roam the land.

The young bulls grow
  and fight among themselves.
The herd increases.

The years pass by
  three autumns,
  three winters,
  three springs,
  three summers.

Slowly a change comes to the Great One.
His strong curving horns
  thicken and roughen.
They lose their shine.
They are scarred and broken
  and the black tips crack.
Then comes the day
  in the dying summer,
  when the earth trembles
  to the fighting of the young bulls.

The earth shakes
   to the poundings of their hoofs.

A young bull dares
   to face the leader.
A young bull dares
   to fight the Chief.

The cows stop feeding
   to watch.
The younger bulls
   form the fighting circle
   and go round and round
   the great ring,
   watching,
   watching.
The two bulls meet
   in the center of the ring.
The meet with a clash
of their strong, shaggy heads.

They push
   they strain,
   their great heads pressing
   their sharp horns locked.

Slowly the old chief gives way.
Slowly his knees bend
   under the power of the younger bull.

He almost falls,
    but with new strength
    he rises again
    to push,
    to strain.

His breath comes panting.
His great heart trembles.
Slowly he backs from the ring.
The circling young bulls part
    to let him go.

Dust clouds the sky
    and hides the sun's face.
Heat lightning flashes.
Thunder echoes
    the bellowings of the bulls.

— 14 —

A defeated herd father
    has two trails to follow.
He can become an old guard
    on the outposts of the herd,
    or he can go by himself.

The defeated herd father
 chooses the lonely trail.
He goes away
 to end his days
 as a proud buffalo should end them.

The herd moves on
 to water, to new grass,
 following the buffalo trails
 following the buffalo ways
 across the Indian lands
 of the Dakotas.

There still are buffalo!

Other Titles in this Series

☐ *Little Herder In Autumn*, by Ann Nolan Clark,
In Navajo and English, $8.95.

☐ *Sun Journey: A Story of Zuni Pueblo*, by Ann Nolan Clark, $8.95.

☐ *Little Boy with Three Names: Stories of Taos Pueblo*,
by Ann Nolan Clark, $8.95.

☐ *Navajo Coyote Tales*, collected by William Morgan, $8.95.

☐ *Wolf Tales: Native American Children's Stories*, edited
by Mary Powell, $8.95. Available Fall 1992.

Ancient City Press
P.O. Box 5401
Santa Fe, New Mexico 87502
(505) 982-8195